# CABO & CORAL REEF EXPLORERS

Snorkeling!

Kayaking!

Surfing!

Living Aloha!

**Dr. Udo Wahn**

**Illustrations by Jennifer Belote**

Copyright 2011 by Dr. Udo Wahn
Library of Congress Control Number: 2010914141
ISBN: 978-0-692-01170-6
1st Edition

This book was printed by Craft Print International Limited, Singapore
Art production: Hang 5 Art & Graphics, 619-276-2676
Copy editing: Karla Olson, BookStudio, www.bookstudiobooks.com

To order additional copies of this book or other books in **The Cabo and Coral Series** go to **www.caboandcoral.com**

Or contact:
Dr Udo Wahn; **udo@caboandcoral.com**

Author and publisher of books with Aloha for the ocean-minded child

# Dedication

To the children of the world: Explore and protect the beautiful treasures of our oceans.

*"We have a stewardship responsibility to maintain healthy, resilient and sustainable oceans, coasts and Great Lakes resources for the benefit of this and future generations."*
- President Barack Obama June 12, 2009

Since this quote, America has suffered the greatest environmental disaster in its history, the Gulf of Mexico oil spill of 2010. Please see how you can help by checking out Surfrider Foundation's website: **www.nottheanswer.org**

# Acknowledgments

**Dr. Greg Hodgson, Sue Chen** and **Mary Luna** of Reef Check Foundation. We appreciate all the useful information that you provided about the beautiful reefs off the coasts of Baja California. www.reefcheck.org

My niece and elementary school teacher, **Viva Sterner**, thank you for reviewing the manuscript.

**Andres, Lea** and **Gina Spagarino**, thank you for your advice and encouragement after listening to my reading of the first draft.

Nice work, **Monterey Bay Aquarium**! The Seafood Watch Program that you have established is brilliant!

# Preface

Cabo and Coral are off on another action packed and fun-filled adventure! Cabo's mom and dad are volunteer divers for Reef Check Foundation. They plan to monitor the beautiful reefs that are just a couple days drive from their home. They will be checking on the status of the fish, shellfish and plant life on two very different reefs. They will be working with the local fishermen to be sure that the reef and its life forms remain sustainable. They'll be snorkeling, kayaking, surfing and living aloha! Dive in as Cabo and Coral have the trip of a lifetime!

After hours of driving down the long desert peninsula, the adventurers stop for lunch.

Their quirky electric-powered van has been running great!

They are giddy with excitement about visiting an offshore island where they will explore an enchanted reef. The blazing desert sun reminds them of how they can use solar energy to be more earth friendly. "It's hotter than a pizza oven out here!" says Cabo.

"Yeah," says Coral, "and these desert plants and rocks are so cool! It looks like we could be on the moon."

Upon arriving on the island, they introduce themselves to the local fishermen. The fishermen welcome them warmly to their island. Cabo cannot contain himself as he spies perfect waves breaking around the point. "It's going off out there!" he exclaims.

Everyone agrees that they must go surfing right away after such a long journey.

"This is juicy! I have been waiting for this all day!" shouts Coral. While getting tubed in the wave, she yells, "Look Cabo, I'm painting the ceiling! Ha!"

"Whoa! I better watch out for those patches of kelp."

"Cabo, your dad told me that the kelp beds provide protection and food for many species on the reef. It is going to be super cool to go snorkeling on the reef later and to see all the marine life up close. Gee, I wonder what lurks down there?"

8

9

Cabo is entranced by the sight of the multicolored reef below him and all the amazing sea life as he slides down the face of the wave.

"The water is so clear, Coral. I can see everything through it. But it's kinda sketchy. The bottom looks really close. Yikes, this would NOT be a good place to fall off!"

10

The next day the family goes out to visit the reef.

The fishermen have banded together to set up areas where no fishing can be done. They regularly monitor the sea life, because they understand that overfishing will deplete the reef of marine creatures.

13

Layla points to a spiny lobster and explains that these lobsters lack large claws. Coral suggests, "That would make it easier for people to take them."

"You're right, Coral," says Layla, "it is super important that people limit the number of lobsters that they take from the reef or they could be gone forever."

Slim tells them about the sea cucumbers. "They are taken, dried and shipped to foreign countries where they are soaked in water and then eaten."

Cabo blurts out, "You have got to be kidding me!"

Coral adds, "Yuk, I'd rather eat a bug!"

Slim reminds them about some of the dangers below. "Look at those spiky sea urchins. They are popular for food like sushi. Be real careful not to step on one."

"That sounds painful!" says Cabo.

Layla tells the kids, "The locals limit their catch to a sustainable level, allowing the reef to remain healthy. By working together for something as important as reef health, they are living the aloha spirit. That means being kind, sharing, and living in harmony with our environment."

After a few days on the island, they journey to the other side of the peninsula. "This is so beautiful and completely different from the other side," says Coral.

Layla tells the kids, "This side has warmer water and is considered sub-tropical. You will be amazed to see how unique the sea life will be on the reefs over here."

BEACH

18

The thick scent of the lush warm sea fills the air as they float over the colorful coral reef.

21

A huge school of giant rays swim by curious about the vibrantly colored kayaks. The family reminds each other about the "Buddy System" of staying close together while snorkeling. They are also mindful of not touching the reef with their fins because they can break the fragile coral.

22

"Hey," says Slim, "Look at the big parrot fish with its powerful teeth biting off the algae-covered dead coral."

"Dad, is that one pooping?" giggles Cabo.

"Yes, the poop is actually ground up digested coral that then becomes sand. One big parrot fish can make up to a ton of sand a year!" explains Slim. "Pollution is a major threat to the reefs around the world. Besides making the water yucky and stinky, the pollution allows too much algae to grow, which covers and kills the coral."

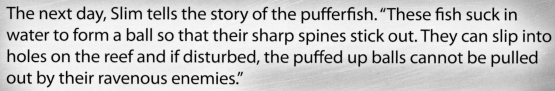

The next day, Slim tells the story of the pufferfish. "These fish suck in water to form a ball so that their sharp spines stick out. They can slip into holes on the reef and if disturbed, the puffed up balls cannot be pulled out by their ravenous enemies."

Layla explains, "Taking fish from here not only gets those who take them into big trouble, but the loss of fish can destroy the reef and the delicate balance needed for the fish, plants, and coral to survive."

"This has been a blast!" exclaims Cabo.

Coral adds, "I can't wait to come back in a couple years to see that the reef remains healthy and to enjoy it again!"

A bountiful table of luscious food awaits them as they say goodbye to their gracious hosts. Only food in plentiful supply has been used for the meal, avoiding anything scarce or endangered.

Slim mentions The Monterey Bay Aquarium's Seafood Watch program. "They list the seafood that is good for you and good for the oceans and seafood to avoid."

As the sun is setting, the explorers reflect on what they learned on this adventure.

Cabo says, "It was fun learning about how important it is to keep our reefs healthy for the benefit of the whole planet."

Coral adds, "We can do this by setting aside Marine Protected Areas and keeping close track of all the cool lifeforms that live on the reefs to ensure that they all thrive."

Slim shouts out, "Hey gang. Let's hit the secret spot and go surfing on the way back home!"

Live aloha!

# Glossary

**Algae** - (noun) - Plantlike organisms usually found in water. They may be green, brown, red or yellow-green.

**Blurt** - (verb) - To say something abruptly or suddenly.

**Endangered** - (adjective) - Threatened with extinction.

**Marine Protected Areas** - Marine areas set aside for conserving natural and cultural marine resources.

**"Painting the ceiling"** - (phrase) - A surfing term, meaning to touch the top of the wave as the curl of the wave flows over your head, as if you were painting the ceiling of the wave.

**Peninsula** - (noun) - A piece of land jutting out into the water, and nearly surrounded by water.

**Predator** - (noun) - One that preys, destroys or devours.

**Sketchy** - (adjective) - Wanting in completeness. In surfing lingo, it refers to a dubious or potentially dangerous situation.

**Spied** - (verb) - To catch sight of.

**Sub-tropical** - (adjective) - Region bordering on the tropical zone.

**Sustainability** - (noun) - The ability to use a resource so that the resource is not depleted or permanently damaged.

**Thrive** - (verb) - To grow vigorously.

**"Tubed"** - (verb) - A surfing term, meaning the wave is curling up all around you, putting you in a tube of water.

**Udo** is an environmental activist serving as a core volunteer for *Surfrider Foundation*. He is an Ob-Gyn doctor living in Del Mar, California. He enjoys surfing, mountain biking, camping and running on the beach. He treasures spending time with his son Paolo "Cabo" and his wife, Aleida.

**Jennifer Belote** is passionate about the environment and conservation. This is a driving force in her life. She is a member of the Wyland Ocean Artist Society, Nature Art Conservancy and *Surfrider Foundation*.